GRATITUDE

notionpress
.com

WIN
GRATITUDE

The Thankful Coat | The Hospital Horse

Notion Press

Old No. 38, New No. 6
McNichols Road, Chetpet
Chennai - 600 031

First Published by Notion Press 2017
Copyright © Blue Orb Pvt. Ltd 2017
All Rights Reserved.

ISBN 978-1-947429-88-8

Book designed by Henu Studio Pvt. Ltd

About The Organisation

The genesis of the name – Blue Orb, lies in the philosophy on which the foundation of the company was laid. Blue represents vastness, limitlessness and the capacity to develop into something great, much like the human potential; and Orb symbolizes the catalyst that brings about the desired change. Embodying the same values that inspire the young and the old to unleash their true potential, our venture was named Blue Orb.

Our conviction is that every child's value system is being shaped every day, every minute and every moment. For this shaping, our team of young innovators and experienced professionals are determined to contribute directly to the physical, intellectual and emotional development of each child inculcating a fundamental value system in each.

Objective

To make value learning an integral part of young developing minds.

Pursuit

To build a generation that can make the right choices, work towards a brighter future and create a winning world.

Our Building Blocks

Our building blocks are aimed at developing and strengthening a young mind's Intelligence Quotient, Emotional Quotient and

Spiritual Quotient. The power to make the right judgment needs courage, which can be obtained from the development of an unclouded foresight and clarity of vision. Our value education module instils the foundations of ethical and cultural thinking in the younger generation, equipping them to make the right decisions throughout life.

What We Do

Our team has developed a set of products and learning methodologies (WIN Value Education Workshops) that can help children, young adults, parents and teachers to develop a fundamentally strong value system. We focus on the eight integral humanitarian values namely Love, Gratitude, Integrity, Courage, Respect, Humility, Trust, and Focus & Commitment.

If you wish to know more about us please.

Visit: www.blueorb.in

Email: info@blueorb.in

Call: +91 8130490580

GRATITUDE

The Thankful Coat

The Thankful Coat

Once upon a time there was a little boy named David. He had a wonderful family and they lived in a beautiful house. David had a little sister and an adorable dog called Rusty. He had nice toys to play with and he went to a good school.

There was just one thing that David did not have; he did know how to be happy. Nothing seemed to make him smile. No matter what his mother, father, sister and even Rusty did, David was always unhappy.

One day, David was sitting on a stool in the backyard feeling sad. A little girl walked right up to him and said, "Hi! I am Sandy. Have you seen the Thankful Coat around here?"

David thought for a moment and said, "A Thankful Coat? I have never heard of anything called a Thankful Coat. And no, I haven't seen one around here."

"Well," said the little girl, "It is the most wonderful coat in the whole world. It makes you feel happy when you wear it."

David asked, "What colour is it?"

"Oh, it is the colour of the rainbow," said Sandy. "Come on, let's look together and then you'll know what it looks like!"

So Sandy and David looked everywhere.

They looked behind the house. They looked under the bushes. They looked all over the backyard. They looked and looked and looked.

Suddenly, they heard a commotion. All the birds, bees, bunnies, squirrels, butterflies and even Rusty were gathered around a large oak tree. There, on a branch, hung a beautiful coat. It was the colour of the rainbow.

"See David, here it is; the Thankful Coat," said Sandy. "Come on, I will help you wear it. You'll see how happy it will make you feel."

So, David held out his arms while Sandy slid the coat over his shoulders.

David rubbed the coat happily and said, "Gee! This coat feels nice and I feel better already, Sandy." All of a sudden, David felt very thankful.

David was thankful for the beautiful blue sky.

He was thankful for his new friend Sandy.

He was thankful for the fun he has with his dog Rusty.

David was thankful for his family. David just felt very thankful.

The more thankful David became, the happier he felt. The happier he became, the bigger his smile grew. David's smile grew bigger and bigger and bigger. Happy thoughts popped up everywhere in his mind. David had found the secret to happiness; it was to wear the Thankful Coat.

David was especially thankful to Sandy. "Sandy, thank you so much for this coat. I feel happy for the first time in my life."

Sandy looked at David and said, "I must leave now David. I have to take this coat to other unhappy children."

"What?" David said in disbelief. "How can you take this coat away, Sandy? I don't want to go back to being unhappy."

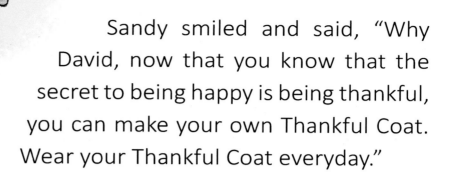

Sandy smiled and said, "Why David, now that you know that the secret to being happy is being thankful, you can make your own Thankful Coat. Wear your Thankful Coat everyday."

"Your Thankful Coat can be an imaginary one and you can make it in any colour you would like it to be. Every day, when you get up, put on your imaginary coat and start to think of all the things that you are thankful for and you will be happy," said Sandy.

David thought for a minute. Then he said, "I think my Thankful Coat would be blue with golden buttons."

"Now, isn't that fun?" asked Sandy smiling.

Sandy hugged David and said, "Goodbye David! I am so glad that you now know the secret to being happy."

David hugged her back and said, "Thank you for sharing the Thankful Coat with me, Sandy. And thank you for teaching me how to make one, too."

After Sandy left, David got out some paper, pencils and crayons. He drew a picture of a coat and coloured it blue. Then he added golden buttons to it. He hung the picture of the Thankful Coat in his room.

The next morning, when David got out of his bed, he looked over at his Thankful Coat, hanging on the wall. Then, he imagined putting it on.

To his surprise, he started feeling happy. The more thankful he became, the happier he felt.

David's life became full of happiness and he remained happy for the rest of his thankful days.

Even you can be as happy as David.

Every morning when you wake up, put on your imaginary Thankful Coat and begin to think about all the things that you have to be thankful for and just like David, you will also have the secret of happiness.

GRATITUDE

The Hospital Horse

The Hospital Horse

Emily's grandparents gifted Emily a rocking, wooden horse for her third birthday. She called him Henry. She could sit on Henry and rock to and fro.

She rocked in the garden.

She rocked in her room. She rocked all around the house.
She loved Henry.

By the time, Emily was six years old, Henry was too small for her. Lying around the house, Henry felt bored and unwanted. The thought of not being useful any longer bothered him to no end.

One day, Henry heard Emily's mummy say, "I think we will send Henry to the hospital." This surprised him. "I know that I am not used, but I am not ill," thought Henry. "Why are they sending me to the hospital?"

Henry was put into a car and driven through the town to the hospital.

At the hospital, he was lifted from the car
and taken into the children's ward.

Here, Henry realized that he had been brought to the hospital so that the children who were getting better and were well enough to play, could play with him.

All the children loved riding him and rocking him, just as Emily had once done.

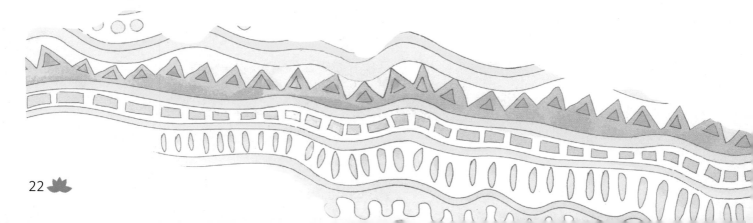

"I think you are going to be busy, happy and useful here, Henry," whispered Emily.

"I think so, too!" smiled Henry.

Henry was thankful to Mummy for having sent him to the hospital and sharing him with so many children.

He was also grateful for his own existence as he helped put a smile on so many children's faces.

Worksheets

What colour would you make your Thankful Coat? What colour would you make the buttons? Go get your crayons and design your own Thankful Coat.

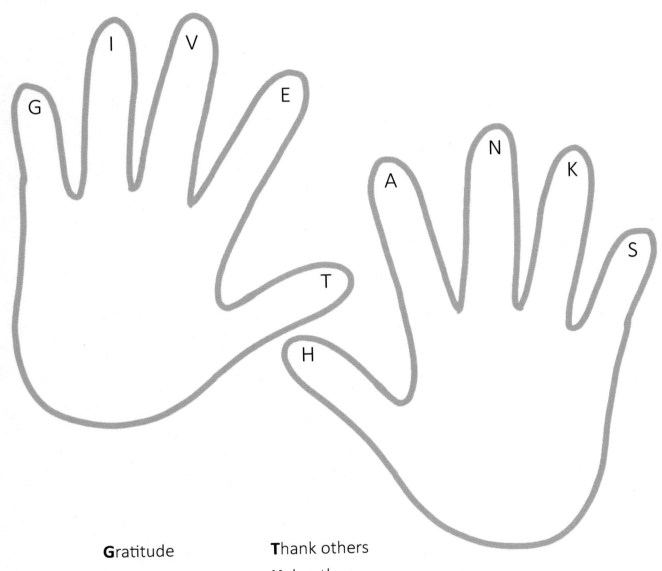

Gratitude is a feeling of thankfulness. See how our hands also mention gratitude. Write the slogan in the hands. Colour them as you wish. These hands will remind you to stay grateful always.

Gratitude

Is

Very

Easy

Thank others

Help others

Appreciate

Notice your blessings

Know your gifts

Serve others

Worksheet II

Gratitude

❧ Colour the pictures and write the following.

I am thankful to my mummy for

_____
_____
_____
_____
_____

I am thankful to my friend for

_____
_____
_____
_____
_____
_____

I am thankful to my teacher for

_____
_____
_____
_____
_____

I am thankful to my neighbour for

_____
_____
_____
_____
_____

Worksheet III

Make a simple 'Thank You' card and present it to someone to whom you are thankful.

Fold

Worksheet IV